NO MORE TRIES

A TRUE STORY

FAIZAN

BLUEROSE PUBLISHERS
India | U.K.

Copyright © Faizan 2025

All rights reserved by the author. No part of this publication may be reproduced, stored in a retrieval system or transmitted in any form or by any means, electronic, mechanical, photocopying, recording or otherwise, without the prior permission of the author. Although every precaution has been taken to verify the accuracy of the information contained herein, the publisher assumes no responsibility for any errors or omissions. No liability is assumed for damages that may result from the use of information contained within.

BlueRose Publishers takes no responsibility for any damages, losses, or liabilities that may arise from the use or misuse of the information, products, or services provided in this publication.

For permissions requests or inquiries regarding this publication, please contact:

BLUEROSE PUBLISHERS
www.BlueRoseONE.com
info@bluerosepublishers.com
+91 8882 898 898
+4407342408967

ISBN: 978-93-6261-747-7

Cover design: Yash Singhal
Typesetting: Namrata Saini

First Edition: January 2025

Contents

Chapter - 1: 160-Kilo Meters 1

Chapter - 2: When I Proposed Her 15

Chapter - 3: Keep My Distance.. 30

Chapter - 4: A Marriage Proposal 38

Chapter - 5: Open Mike Performance............................. 51

Chapter - 1

160-kilo meters

10th February, 2024. (Saturday)

Both buses started their trip, but they were running late like it often happens with wedding processions. Today, we were heading from Delhi to Chandpur for Shiraz Mama's wedding procession. One bus was designated for gentlemen, and the other for ladies. It's imperative to have a sensible man accompanying the women, hence my compulsion to board the ladies' bus. Wait! Was it compulsion or was it my choice? Obviously, It was my choice to sit on the ladies' bus because there was someone very special on that bus.

The traffic on the small road in Jaitpur was a mess, turning a short journey from Makki Masjid to Khadar, which is less than 1 km away, into a whole hour of travel.

It was already 8 p.m., and the bus hadn't even exited the colony, although it had to cover 160 km still. All the wedding guests were extremely disturbed — children were crying, women's makeup was ruined, people were turning red with anger. But there was one person who seemed unaffected by it all, and that was me.

The girl sitting next to me on the adjacent seat was my peace, and spending time with her was nothing short of a blessing for me. Now I don't care about the traffic, whether we would stuck here all night, the more the traffic, the more time I would get to spend with her. Perhaps some people were only worried because Faizan wasn't worried.

There was just one thing bothering me, and that was her melancholic face. She looks even more beautiful when she smiles, but that smile is missing somewhere. Both buses weren't moving forward but rather inching along. All the guys got off the bus to help clear the traffic so that the bus could get out of this mess. But here I was, inside the bus, trying to entertain her with my nonsensical jokes. The chaos of traffic coming through the bus window, the noise of children, the commotion of women, everything seemed pleasant to me as long as her face was in front of me.

I don't know if she's being entertained by my nonsense jokes or if my words are irritating her even more. I wanted to know what was on her mind, so jokingly, I said, 'Excuse me! I'm going to the other bus.' Perhaps now she'll stop me from leaving. That's what I hoped. However, she said something entirely different, "All right then, go ahead," and with those words, she even cleared the way for me to leave. She probably didn't realize what she had just said. I got off the bus, but I didn't return. How could I, after she had permitted me to leave? But I had boarded the ladies' bus solely because of her. I entered the gentlemen's bus.

The bus finally cleared the traffic, and the cool breeze started blowing in through the windows, carrying with it a sense of relief. Soft music began playing in the background, bringing a calm atmosphere after all the commotion. The pleasant journey had begun, but I didn't like all of this because of her absence. Perhaps a decent person would have called to ask where I was, and why I hadn't returned to the bus. But it seemed like she was waiting for me to leave.

Ten minutes later, my phone rang.

Incoming call from "**Hoor Ain**"

Hoor Ain: Hello Faizan, where are you? I can't see you on the bus.

Faizan: I've switched to the other bus.

Hoor Ain: Why?

Faizan: Because you asked me to go.

Hoor Ain: No, I didn't say that.

Faizan: Yes, you did. That's why I didn't come back.

Hoor Ain: No, I didn't say that. Now we'll be bored here, why did you go there? That's not right.

Faizan: All right, I'll come there.

I replied and disconnected the call.

OMG! I can't believe it. She called me. A smile spread across my face. So much happiness...

She finally called me. After her call, it felt like I couldn't wait to go back to her on that bus. But her bus was ahead, and ours was behind. Now I needed both buses to stop so I could reach her. Faisal was on the other bus. Faisal is my cousin, Rihana Phuppo's son. When I arrived on the gentlemen's bus, he had switched to the ladies' bus. I called Faisal and said, "We're approaching the toll booth, stop the bus after crossing the toll." When our bus stopped at the toll booth, I got off and ran a little ahead. The other bus, where my destination awaited, was standing there. On the highway, I was the only guy who was running amidst the cars, dressed in a suit, running like a horse putting in all my efforts. I felt like Krish, all I had left to do was fly.

At the toll booth, the wedding guests who had arrived earlier in cars were waiting for the buses, and they noticed me running. They were probably thinking, "Why is he running on the road?" When they saw the bus, they gestured to go. The bus was approaching, and

I was almost there, suddenly it started moving again and picking up speed. Faisal, who was on the phone call with me, I told him, "Hey, stop the bus, you fool!" Finally, the bus stopped, I ran and boarded it.

As soon as I entered the bus, everyone greeted me with cheers, and then the two-hour journey passed with her by my side.

My elder uncle's wedding happened almost 10 years ago, but today it was my younger uncle's turn. For the past three days, we've all been at grandma's house, sometimes with ceremonies like the Mandha, sometimes with Haldi rituals; something or the other is always happening. Today was the wedding procession. My aunt Zahra is my mother's sister, but her daughter, who is just two and a half months older than me, and yes her name is **Hoor Ain**. I feel like I'm experiencing the golden period of my life, getting this opportunity to spend so much time with her. The wedding happened today, and the reception is in two days, which is great because she'll be staying here for the next two days as well.

11th February, 2024. (Sunday)

The wedding procession returned at 6 AM. Our house is right next to Grandma's. She went from Grandma's house to ours with my younger sister. So, what am I doing here? I'm also heading back home.

While saying something to me, she slipped out, "Yeah bro."

"I'm not your bro," I whispered. Finally, today, I said that I'm not your bro. In return, she didn't say anything. After changing the dress, we arrived at Grandma's house. A ritual called "Kheer Chatai" was ongoing. There was dancing and everything was going fine, but the real fun began when we all gathered in a room to play a game called "Ek machli, pani me gai, chapaak". I found myself looking more at her happy face. Since everyone was seated, I couldn't stare at her as much as I wanted to, but whenever I looked her way, I wished I could continue looking.

Well, it's now 3 a.m., and we boys have returned home to sleep. She is still at Grandma's house.

12th February, 2024. (Monday)

Good morning. It's 10:00 in the morning, and I want to sleep a little more, but it'll be difficult to fall asleep now. Today will be a good day. There's the Mandha ceremony in the evening, and tomorrow is the reception. I'm going to Grandma's house for breakfast. Oh wait, I forgot to mention something very special about yesterday. Last night, Rizan recited a poem, claiming he wrote it himself. Rizan is Hoor Ain's younger brother.

After he recited his poem, I got the chance to share mine. I recited a poem I had written myself, in front of everyone, Hoor Ain was also there.

Arz kya hai. Gor farmaiye.

Mohobbat ke sode me Sara hamara hi khasara tha.....

Bda be reham tha Mera Sanam mere Marne pr bhi uska kuch na jara tha.....

Use khabar tak na thi kitne aansu bahe mere.....

Mere ashqo ko lekin gina ja rha tha.....

Uski muskurahat ki aanch se mai phir pighal gya.....

Mai be wajah hi apne ashq gine jaa raha tha....

Wah! Wah! Wah! Everyone praised me. Hoor Ain also praised me and left. She is so innocent. I was only talking about her but she will never understand.

After having breakfast, she had gone home to get some clothes, but we had breakfast together from the same plate. She mentioned she'd be back by 3 p.m.

It's already 6 o'clock, and she hasn't returned yet. I'm off to the gym now.

When I returned home from the gym, I saw a girl in a navy blue frock. Silver-colored earrings adorned her ears, and a silver dupatta draped from one shoulder to the other. Around her neck, there was a delicate golden necklace. She was looking at herself in the mirror while arranging her hair. I felt like saying,

"You look exceptionally lovely today, Hoor Ain. If anyone hasn't seen an Engle, they should see you today."

But I refrained from speaking such words to her, nor did I compliment her in front of her, fearing she might think I was flirting with her. It would be strange to say such things, so I remained silent. To be very honest, It's not that she isn't beautiful, but she's not as good as I think she is.

Anyway, I'm heading to Grandma's house now. There's a lot of work to do; the Mandha ceremony is today, and Uncle's been calling me repeatedly.

13th February, 2024. (Tuesday)

Today is the wedding reception, and this is the last function. After today's event, she will go back to her home in Abul Fazal. I wish she could stay here for a few more days. Hoor Ain had already left; she went to the beauty parlor with the bride to get ready for the reception. She went to Daryaganj, to some big parlor. I'm also heading to the marriage hall to oversee the arrangements.

I arrived at the banquet hall at 7 p.m. after changing clothes, but she still hadn't arrived; she was still on her way.

A girl in a black saree is approaching. Some of her hair is curly, and it falls on her face. She's wearing a white pearl necklace around her neck, and there are some pearls in her hair too. She's about 5 feet 6 inches tall. Yes, that's Hoor Ain. She's completely changed. Just like always, I want to compliment her, but I don't. She didn't even come near me. Well, today I'm also wearing an off-white kurta with a brown shawl. Many people complimented me. She could have said once, "You're looking good, Faizan," but she didn't. She didn't even stray near me.

The wedding is over, Thank God, everything went well. It's 4:30 in the morning now, and I'm going to sleep. My friends were also at the wedding today— Shahnawaz, Arsalan, Javed, Ibrar, Sayyad, and Sajid. Javed has known Hoor Ain for almost 10 years, but he saw her for the first time today. I often used to tell Javed about Hoor Ain.

The bad thing is that today Hoor Ain didn't talk to me at all; she didn't even mention my name once. She never says, "Come, let's take a photo together," or asks why I'm sitting alone, or makes any excuse to come and talk to me. Well, why would she? She doesn't love me. If I love her, I'll have to do everything.

Yesterday, she was talking to me so nicely, but today, she didn't even look at me. Well, she never looks at me. I'm the one who always goes to her to seek her attention, then I feel happy when she talks to me. But today, it hurts me, and now I don't think I should talk to her again. The function ended, she went home, we also went home, and now it's back to normal life.

Normally, we don't talk much on WhatsApp or calls. We don't share personal matters. It was the wedding atmosphere that gave us a chance to spend time together again, and just like every time, I felt weak and tried to get close to her. Although I knew I would be in pain later when she would go away.

We live in a three-bedroom flat with my family. My parents, one brother, one sister, and me. My father is a property dealer who manages to earn about 20 to 30 thousand rupees per month. My younger sister helps with household chores after completing her graduation, and my youngest brother, who quit his job, is now involved in trading. Even fulfilling the basic needs of the house is difficult with my father's income, and his eldest son dreams of marrying a princess. Yes, I'm talking about myself.

Alongside my graduation, I had started working, being the eldest son of the family, I was always concerned about the state of the household. I've changed many jobs so far, and switched fields countless times—sometimes I'm a customer executive, sometimes a wedding organizer, sometimes a BPO trainer, sometimes an English teacher, or sometimes I feel like I should start a business. Thank God, I have many talents and skills, but I lack perfection in any one field.

After doing so much, I've finally reached a decision. I've started a course in Data Science, and I hope to earn a salary of 1 lakh per month after completing it. If that happens, perhaps I can propose to Hoor Ain. With this hope, I've started dreaming again. But now, I don't have much time left.

On the other hand, if we talk about Hoor Ain's family, they are financially strong. Her father is a businessman, and Hoor Ain is a physiotherapist doctor, working in a hospital. I have no interest in their money; rather, this is the biggest challenge for me. If this financial difference wasn't so significant, perhaps things would be easier.

I'm not exceptionally handsome, but some girls are crazy about me. Last time when I was a soft skills trainer, some girls in my office liked me, and I never hesitated to flirt back. But I felt it was a sin, so I repented and decided not to have a girlfriend. If I liked a girl, I would marry her directly. I was trying to forget Hoor Ain even then. But when Hoor Ain appears in front of me, I forget that I want to forget her. And when the thought of marriage comes to my mind, I only see Hoor Ain.

Anyway, leave all these things. Tomorrow, I'm going to Abul Fazal where Hoor Ain lives. Let's see what happens.

15th February, 2024. (Thursday)

Shiraz mama has rented a flat at Abul Fazal, near Hoor Ain's house. I came to Abdul Fazal with Shiraz mama to arrange the furniture for their new flat, but first, we went to Zahra Aunty's house. I didn't even properly look at Hoor Ain, and now I don't even feel like talking to her, just as she didn't talk to me the day before yesterday at the reception. She asked me for water, but I kept staring at the turned-off TV as if there were some incredibly interesting movie scene playing. I kept ignoring her voice as if I couldn't hear anything amidst the noise of the DJ. She brought water and placed it on the table, then went to her room. After she left, I took a deep breath, drank some water, and went outside.

16th February, 2024. (Friday)

Today I was getting bored so I went Rihana Phuppo's house with my mother. Aunt Rihana is Faisal's mother, the same Faisal who stopped the bus for me. I used to share my secrets with him; later, I realized he blabbers everything to anyone, so now I'm a bit cautious. Everyone was sitting comfortably, gossiping about others, when suddenly, I don't know what happened, but people started worrying about my marriage.

"I'll arrange his marriage." Uncle Den said.

"No, absolutely not." In a fraction of a second, I replied.

"Do it wherever he wants" someone from behind said.

"Who is she? Are you talking about Kinza?" Uncle Den asked.

"Not with Kinza, everyone agrees there, except Faizan; his choice is somewhere else," Aunt Rihana replied.

I was shocked that these people were talking about me so much like this.

"Then where is his choice?" Uncle Den asked.

"He likes his Kala's daughter" Aunt Rihana whispered into my mom's ear.

"Whom you are talking about?" Mom asked.

"We all know about his choice, **Don't be a pit in the mango.**" Aunt Rihana said sharply.

"With Hoor Ain, with Hoor Ain," Aunt Rihana again whispered to my mom in a very soft voice.

After hearing Hoor Ain's name, my mother's expression was worth seeing.

'If you can make it happen, then go ahead and do it there.'" With this statement, Mom returned to home.

I was still shocked about all this conversation whatever they did. What insolence is this, how did Aunt Rihana know about my preferences? I only shared it with Faisal; how did Aunt Rihana find out, and even if she did, why did she say it in front of my mother? I'm getting very angry. I don't want to tarnish her name by associating it with mine; people always make something out of nothing. Many questions were running through my mind. Now, when I go home, I hope Mom doesn't ask me any questions about this stuff.

Being away from Hoor Ain has made life seem dull; in my free time, I spend it watching her photos and videos. I need to do something in my free time So that there's some money left in my pocket; it's completely drained now.

The amazing thing is, Faheem bhai's wedding is also in four days, the joy in this is that I'll get another chance to spend time with Hoor Ain during the wedding festivities. But I shouldn't be too happy right now; I should stick to what I was doing—maintaining distance. I'll go to the wedding, and Hoor Ain will be there too, but I won't talk to her much. I won't keep turning to look at her, won't crack jokes to make her laugh, and overall, I'll keep my distance from her.

Chapter - 2

When I Proposed Her

I don't remember when I first fell in love with Hoor Ain. As far back as I can recall from my childhood memories, I've always loved her. During parties, when kids would fight over getting ice cream, I used to pick flowers from the stage for her. I learned to ride a bicycle so that she could sit behind me on the back seat. I used to remember jokes to make her laugh.

I must have been around 10 or 12 years old when I started to like her. Back then, I was quite skinny, and she was a bit chubby. I was a bit dark-skinned, and she wasn't extremely fair either. But the good thing was that we were very close to each other back then. I considered her my friend, or perhaps she was a very good friend of mine.

We used to live in Mustafabad, and she has always lived in Abdul Fazal. Her house was about 25 km away from mine, so I couldn't go to meet her alone. But I would try my best to grow up quickly so that I could go to her house alone someday, whenever I felt like seeing her.

I often went to her house by auto-rickshaw with my parents. My heart would beat faster as we approached Jamia University; it was a different kind of joy. I had fallen in love with her streets too. I could only see Hoor Ain when we came to Abdul Fazal with Mom on school holidays, during Eid, or on occasions of joy or sorrow. And I would eagerly await these opportunities. Sometimes, they would also come to our house.

I would feel heartbroken when it was time to return home from there, but I had to go home anyway.

The fear haunted me, a fear that perhaps this childishness, these emotions, this connection would not fade away as I grew older. With time, these feelings, these sensations, would they not diminish? But instead, they grew stronger. She began to appeal to me so much that she probably didn't even like herself as much as I liked her.

I remember Hoor Ain used to stick with me during weddings and parties. Sometimes, she would share small secrets with me, and when I wasn't around, she used to ask about me.

It became my routine to protect Hoor Ain from bullies before going to bed every night. Sometimes, in the process of protecting her, I would end up hurting myself. All of this was just a part of my dreams, that I used to watch with my open eyes. In reality, I could do nothing to her. Fate never gave me a chance to do something special for her.

The dream of riding a bicycle with Hoor Ain sitting behind finally came true one day, and that moment was better than driving a Rolls-Royce.

Once, I wore a blue coat to a reception, feeling grand as it was the first time I wore one. I bought it from Jama Masjid for Rs. 300, accompanied by my mother. After putting on the coat, some cousins started teasing me, calling me "baje wala," which translates to 'outdated' in English. I felt upset, but Hoor Ain stood there, saying, "No, Faizan, you look good. Don't pay attention to their words. **Hoor Ain praised me, and I forgot my cousin's comments.**"Why should I care about others' opinions when you're praising me?" I thought in my mind. That one line of hers made me happy for three days. Perhaps even more.

At that time, I hadn't even thought about proposing to Hoor Ain or confessing my feelings. It didn't seem appropriate for a 14- or 15-year-old, so I kept everything in my heart. I told myself to be patient and wait for the right moment.

Once, I asked Hoor Ain, "I have a friend who likes his cousin. What should he do?" Hoor Ain replied, "Right now, he should focus on his studies. This age is for learning."

During those days, I didn't share my secrets with anyone, not even with my closest friend Javed, about Hoor Ain.

Since the fourth grade, I attended the government school, but Javed got admitted in the seventh grade; previously, he was just an innocent child from a private school. He asked me if I would be his friend for real, and I agreed. He said, "From today onwards, we'll share everything, like lunch boxes and pocket money." Being a student of the private school he didn't know that there were no desks in government schools, so we had to bring a mat from home to sit on. He also didn't know how to deal with clever students and guest teachers.

I was well-trained to face every challenge of the government school, knowing which wall could be climbed to escape or which period could be skipped. I helped Javed face every challenge, while I was also excelling in my studies because I believed that education was the key to becoming worthy of Hoor Ain.

Hoor Ain studied in a good private school. It had been a long time since I silently loved her. I felt like it was time to tell her and speak up my feelings. But how could I? Every time I planned to go to her house, I couldn't muster the courage to speak up.

Once, I met her at a wedding, and she said to me, "Where were you? I asked your mother about you. Look, I've got a phone, and a contact number. Call me soon on my number." She had bought a Samsung 3310, her first mobile phone. I already had a phone, so I saved her number in my phone and my mind. I felt like I had hit the jackpot; now I could talk to Hoor Ain whenever I wanted. Why was she so special to me? My love was at its peak at that time; I didn't even look at any other girl. I didn't want any other girl's name associated with mine. As time passed, I felt like she was drifting away from me. I decided that I had to propose to her; I was already 17 years old.

Finally, I messaged Hoor Ain on Facebook.

[Chat box]

Me: Hello Hoor Ain, Don't tell anyone, Hoor Ain.

Hoor Ain, a few days ago, I told you that I love someone. It's you. I love you very much.

(Finally, after years, I proposed to her that day, but I did it in such a pathetic way. I had thought of doing it differently, but in the end, I did it like that. What a shame.)

I checked my mobile; her reply had come.

Hoor Ain: I am sorry, Faizan. I don't have any such feelings for you. And don't worry, I won't share this with anyone.

Faizan: Why, Hoor Ain? Why are you refusing? Do you think I'm just flirting? What made you refuse after all?

Hoor Ain: I didn't think about it; I just refused.

(What else was left to ask? My entire life had passed by thinking about her, and she didn't even think once before refusing.)

Kyaaaa... itnaaa.... bura... hu mai maa...

I felt sad, but I wasn't disheartened because I was mentally prepared for this reply. I had a feeling that she might say something like that, and I also knew what to do next.

I should propose to her again, and explain it to her properly so she understands me.

I went to her house, and her reaction was as if nothing had happened, completely normal.

Anyway, after a few days, I started saying Hi-hello again to Hoor Ain, and one day, amid our normal conversation, I spoke up.

[Chat Box]

Me: Is everything fine at home? What's Zahra Aunty doing?

Hoor Ain: Everything's fine. Mom is cooking.

Me: I love you.

(This was completely unexpected; I suddenly blurted it out.)

Hoor Ain: Faizan, I refused you before, and I don't want to hurt you, but I like someone else. So please don't say it again like this. Okay?

Me: Who is he?

Hoor Ain: I can't tell that.

Me: Does he like you too?

Hoor Ain: Maybe. I don't know. If he doesn't, he will. So please don't talk to me like this again.

Me: Okay! May God fulfill your wish.

I sincerely prayed for her above and ended the chat.

(This was when I had entered the 11th standard, and so had she. She had chosen the Science stream in a school in Noida, while I ended up in a rough school with a commerce stream including Maths.)

Wait, how could this be? She couldn't possibly like someone else. I had never entertained the thought of someone else's name being associated with mine. How could she say that her life belonged to someone else? Is my life over now? My mind was swirling with questions, pulling me into despair. I couldn't bear what she had said, but I couldn't do anything except endure it, and even that seemed impossible as tears welled up in my eyes. I couldn't even explain that feeling now.

Maybe I was late in telling her. It was such a shock that it shook me to the core.

Javed understood; that I came to school today after being beaten by Mom. He continuously asked about the matter behind my sadness.

That day, for the first time, I told Javed everything about Hoor Ain.

"You didn't tell me before, even though we've been together all these years, now you're telling me," Javed said.

"I never felt this much pain before. All hopes seem shattered in an instant. How could she even imagine someone else? I was mentally prepared for so many challenges, but I never expected this." I replied

"I've loved her since before she even knew the meaning of love, and now she suddenly says she likes someone else, and I don't even know if that guy likes her back or not."

Anyway, God gave me patience with time, and I eventually returned to normal after some time. I thought I would go to Abul Fazal and talk to Hoor Ain about this. But fate had its way. When I faced her, I couldn't say anything; I was tongue-tied. But one day on

Facebook, I asked again, "Hoor Ain, what about that guy you were talking about?"

"Whom you are talking about?" She asked confusedly.

"The guy you used to like, you said once." I memorized her.

"That's canceled, forget about him." She replied.

(After a long time, I realized that she used to like no one, perhaps she lied to me so that I forget about her.)

I didn't ask anything further, why it was canceled, what happened. I started to see a glimmer of hope again. I started talking to Hoor Ain again. Things normalized, so I thought I would give it one last try, and express my feelings properly, maybe she would understand me, and she would have to understand. Her message is still in my chat box from the last time I proposed to her.

[Chat box, 10th February 2016. chat with Hoor Ain]

Faizan: Hi, sorry to disturb you again. I thought I should stop thinking about you, but I couldn't resist without seeing you.

Hoor Ain: Don't say that. Okay.

Me: I thought I would meet you and talk, but I didn't get the chance. Even if I did, I didn't have the courage. If it didn't happen in 8-9 years, how could it happen now? Hoor Ain I love you very, very, very much, sincerely.

If you find any shortcomings in me, tell me, I'll change, I will become better than this. I just want to marry you.

Hoor Ain: Faizan, stop it. I never thought like that about you. I don't want to hurt you. That's why I refused in the beginning.

Me: Yes, that's true. You'll find someone better than me. But no one can take care of you more than me.

Hoor Ain: Don't say anything like that again, ever...please. And I'm very serious, okay?

Me: Now it's your turn to speak. Say whatever you want.

Hoor Ain: I'll only say No!, No! and No! Don't say anything like this again next time...please.

Me: You said you are serious, do you think I am joking?

Hoor Ain: Whatever it is, end this conversation now. Don't send me any messages like this again. Final.

Faizan: Okay, final. Sorry, but if you ever change your mind, just tell me without hesitation.

Chat ended.

I was only speaking whatever I had to say without listening to her. I was doing this so that I would never regret not expressing my feelings in a better way. That's why I tried my best to express my feelings and I could not do it better than this. If she still didn't understand me, she might never understand. However, nowadays I realize how awful the method I chose. But there was innocence in it; my heart was pure.

It's been 8 years since these messages, but reading them again today feels like I'm being humiliated anew. After such humiliation, no respectable person would even look back at that person, but love endures great humiliation. I thought now I should look for another girl to forget her, but I couldn't find a girlfriend as per my choice. Even leaving Hoor Ain wasn't in my control. After all, she's the one who's somewhere always visible, as she's my Khala's daughter. Then to top it all off, I shifted to Jaitpur from Mustafabad with my family, close to Hoor Ain's home.

17th February, 2024,. at 2:52 AM

It's been nearly 8 years now, and she must have forgotten all these things by now. Since then, I have never proposed to her again. I have never let my love be known to her. Perhaps I should have kept seeing these messages from time to time so that I wouldn't make the mistake of falling in love with her again. But when she appears before me, I forget all the past. I even stopped talking to her occasionally, and started ignoring her completely, but what was the use? I was just pretending to ignore her; my mind was always on her.

16th February, 2024. (Saturday)

Shiraz mama has rented a flat at Abul Fazal. Since 2:30, we've been at Shiraz mama's flat to arrange furniture and kitchen set-up, me, Shiraz mama, aunt, and Hoor Ain. Hoor Ain arrived at 3:30 PM from home with lunch, but we didn't have any conversation, and I'm trying not to talk much with Hoor Ain. Even if we don't talk, it feels good when she's around.

After some time, Hoor Ain left for her home, and her mom came to Shiraz Mama's flat. Now the discussion here is about Hoor Ain's proposal. Someone has mentioned a boy for her, he seems good, earning a salary of 2 lakhs, and so on. Well, I don't care about it, it's just that my body feels uneasy.

I was typing all this when Mom came into my room and said, "What are you speaking nowadays with people?"

"What are you talking about?" I replied.

"What did you say to Rihana yesterday? What was she saying?" Mom asked.

"Her mind is messed up, I've never said anything to her," I replied.

"Then why was she saying that you like Hoor Ain, etc.?" Mom asked.

"I don't know, I've never said anything like that to her. I never talked to her about this, nor do I have any such intention to marry Hoor Ain." I replied to Mom and covered up the matter, the same matter when people were talking about my marriage.

"Tell Rihana tomorrow not to bring up this topic again," Mom advised me.

"Yes, I'll talk to her," I replied.

"If our son were worthy, we would have discussed it. If anyone hears about it, it will create unnecessary talk. The girl is good, but we are not equal in her standards," Mom started explaining to me.

"Mom, don't worry, I don't even want to go there. I'll explain to Aunt Rihana too not to bring up this topic again and I have no such feelings about Hoor Ain" I assured my Mom.

Listening to Mom's words and seeing my condition, made me cry from inside, I felt like resting my head in Mom's lap and crying for a while, but let it be for now. I could not express my pain to my Mom it would trouble her.

18th February, 2024. (Sunday)

Sunday, which means a fun day. We went to play cricket, although I'm not good at it, but all my friends go, so it's fun to play with them. Let's see who's come to play today. No one showed up to play today, hence I decided to go somewhere else.

I've arrived at Govind Puri at Javed's flat. Ibrar, Javed, Sayyad, and Sajid live here; their workplace is nearby, and they also make videos for their channel "Three Square" together, which is why they rented a flat here.

The condition of the flat is always the same: blankets, sheets, and pillows, all lying where they were last time. Some dishes are dirty, and there's leftover food in others; four Chapties are wrapped in a piece of paper. Charger cables are tangled with each other. Javed isn't at the flat; he's gone to meet Aisha, his love once. Sayyad has gone to visit Delhi with his Facebook Friend, who has come from Bengal to meet him. Sajid is at his home. They'll all be back soon. Only Ibrar is here who opened the door after 15 minutes of knocking the door.

I first met Ibrar and Sayyad at the railway station when we were going on a trip to Mussoorie; Javed already knew them. The first meeting was as if we had known each other for ages or were childhood friends.

After spending the whole day with friends, I've returned home.

Chapter - 3

Keep my Distance

Who can give me the best suggestion right now? What should I do about Hoor Ain? Well, for now, the best suggestion is that I should go to sleep. I have to attend Faheem Bhai's wedding tomorrow. Hoor Ain will also be there. It's obvious she's also a cousin, but I have no intention of seeing her or talking to her. I think I should entrust everything to God and maintain distance from Hoor Ain until I find a way to become worthy of her. But my intentions weaken greatly when she's in front of me, but I'll try to keep myself away from her.

19th February, 2024. (Monday)

Two cars are about to leave from Abul Fazal for Charthawal today for Faheem bhai's wedding. We'll be leaving from Jaitpur soon.

Upon reaching there, I shouldn't get too emotional, shouldn't joke too much, and must maintain distance from Hoor Ain. Finally, we reached Charthawal after a 3-hour journey. Hoor Ain looks very beautiful, but let her look beautiful; what do I care? I shouldn't look towards her.

I spent half an hour with her and all the planning went haywire. I couldn't control my jokes, and couldn't resist looking at her repeatedly; her behavior toward me was normal. I don't want to talk to her. The problem is I can't stop myself from falling in love with her when she's around. I can't become stern, but I'm trying my best. And my efforts seem to be failing.

We all left Charthawal for Khatauli around 12:30 AM, the bride's home. When we arrived here, everyone was fast asleep. We woke them up with a bang, and after a while, we also went to sleep.

20th February, 2024. (Tuesday)

Today the wedding procession will come from Charthawal, and we plan to return to Charthawal along with the procession.

A tale of the wedding hall: Zahra Aunt told me, "Look, Faizan, Mahak is standing behind you, looking quite beautiful." Mahak is a beautiful girl from distant relatives. About two years ago, I had asked my mother to arrange my marriage with Mahak because I thought that Hoor Ain would get married soon somewhere else, and I would be left alone. So, it's better to marry a beautiful girl like Mahak before Hoor Ain's wedding. But my mother didn't consider it because of some reason. Mahak is indeed a beautiful girl, to tell the truth, even more beautiful than Hoor Ain, but it's a different matter. No one seems as good to me as Hoor Ain. Hoor Ain is different; I can't compare her with any other girl. Seeing her face gives me a different peace. Anyway, I was talking about Mahak. I looked back; Mahak was standing in a white suit. I told Aunt, "Yes, she looks good". As I gazed at Mahak, suddenly Hoor Ain passed by her, and my gaze involuntarily followed its path. Again I said, "Yes, Aunt Hoor Ain does indeed look very lovely. I'm sorry, Mahak."

With the wedding procession, we all have also arrived in Charthawal. Hoor Ain is sitting on a chair on the sofa, I am sitting on the sofa next to hers, and this is the bride's room. Everyone else is sitting in the same room, and gossip is going on. Hoor Ain has a cup of tea in her hand, and I am dipping my biscuits in the same cup. In my hand is a packet of chips which we are sharing, but whenever she takes out chips from the packet, I look at her with a playful gaze, as if saying, "How did you take chips without my permission?" And she laughs and takes out chips again. If only we could share things like this for our whole life, how better it would be, I thought.

21st February, 2024. (Wednesday)

Today is the reception, and I'm wearing a mehndi-colored kurta with a green shawl. It looks very nice, and two or three people have already complimented me. But Hoor Ain doesn't seem to like it; even if the whole world praises me, she can't. And I only like hearing compliments from her; it feels good when she speaks in my favor.

Well, she is wearing a green frock, the Same color as mine, and looking beautiful, but I will also not compliment her.

After a few while, She came to me with a beautiful smile and said.

"You are looking good, This kurta looks very nice on you, and the shawl too. Badnam Shayar"

You are also looking beautiful. I said.

"Thank you" she replied.

"Badnaam Shayar", what a unique name she suggested to me, but everything looks good when it belongs to her. I like the name she gave me for the day. I had to dance in the corner to digest the happiness that I got when she praised me like this.

Before leaving for home after the wedding reception, everyone started playing games. They played "musical chairs" where chairs were arranged in a circle, and when the music played, everyone had to walk around the chairs. When the music stopped, they had to quickly find a chair to sit on. Whoever couldn't find a chair was eliminated from the game.

There came a moment when Hoor Ain and I were both walking ahead and when the music stopped, there was only one chair in front of us. Either she could sit on it, or I could. In a split second, I quickly sat on the chair, and Hoor Ain was eliminated. Well, love has its place, and the game has its place, so I eliminated Hoor Ain from the game. Anyway, the game lasted only for 15 minutes, and then we all headed home for Delhi.

Now, from tomorrow, the boring life will begin. You must have realized by now how determined I am, how much I had thought I would stay away from Hoor Ain, not talk to her, not even look at her, and see what I have done.

22nd February, 2024. (Thursday)

Today was a bit dull, struggled through my class, barely managed to continue with gym, and spent the rest of the day just lying around. There's nothing to do, no friends nearby, no other companions, and at the moment, there's no desire to do anything either.

At 11:45 p.m., Nadeem's call comes in. He says he's at Javed's flat with Shahbaz brother, asking me to join them. Nadeem is a school friend, living in Mustafabad, without a girlfriend. In childhood, his engagement was with his uncle's daughter, but it ended in youth.

Shahbaz is both my cousin and friend. Shahbaz had his own separate story. Initially, it seemed his sorrow was greater than mine because the girl he used to like had married. Then one day, a Ma'am came into his life, and his love life also settled. At 11:45 pm, Nadeem called, and by 11:59 pm, I reached Javed's flat from Jaitpur to Govind Puri. At home, it's said that Javed has urgent work on his laptop so I have to go. It doesn't feel good to lie, but sometimes you have to. I've also brought food packed from home for these scoundrels. They asked me to bring 6 chapatis, I brought 10, but still, I was hungry.

Nadeem is adamant about going home, he insists he must leave by 2:00 a.m. Javed, Ibrar, Sayyad, and Sajid have created an atmosphere by telling horror stories related to this flat, making Nadeem not want to stay here anymore. Nadeem's face is worth seeing; I got a stomach ache from laughing. At first, even I thought these guys were telling the truth, but later I understood they were just pulling a prank, but poor Nadeem is terrified by these horror stories. It was very difficult to stop Nadeem from going home; he was so scared that he might get a heart attack.

We managed to stop Nadeem from going home, but all night they kept scaring him, sometimes by dropping utensils, sometimes by playing horror sounds.

At 3:30 a.m., Javed got hungry, so we all went to Shaheen Bagh to eat biryani. When we decided to sleep at 4 a.m., Nadeem started saying,

"Now it's morning, you guys, I won't let you sleep now. You didn't let me sleep all night, now scare me as much as you want, and now let the ghost come."

Nadeem was over-exited with the morning.

Javed wanted to sleep because he had to go to the office in the morning, but now Nadeem wasn't letting anyone sleep. There were two rooms in the flat; Javed went to the other room.

A little while later, the lights went off, and footsteps could be heard along with the tinkling of Payal's anklets. Cham.. cham... cham... We all fell silent as the utensils started falling on their own, and strange sounds of a girl's scream began, either crying or the most terrifying were those footsteps approaching with a tinkling sound. I knew Javed was behind all this, but Nadeem's courage faltered.

Nadeem's heartbeats accelerated; he covered himself completely with the blanket, his breaths became faster, and he lost all consciousness. His condition was such that it resembled someone having a heart attack.

I got scared seeing Nadeem's terrible condition; I turned on the lights. Javed had created such a dangerous atmosphere that Nadeem was on the verge of a heart attack. Some were splashing water on Nadeem's face, others were calling out to him, but he was taking deep, labored breaths.

When his breathing became somewhat normal, we felt relieved, but it took him 5 to 7 minutes to regain consciousness. Everyone fell asleep by 7 in the morning, and when I woke up, it was time for the Friday prayer, around 12:30 p.m. I reached home on time, but I don't know about Shahbaz and Nadeem, whether they attended the prayer or not; they had to go back to Mustafabad, to their homes.

Chapter - 4

A Marriage Proposal

24th FebrUary, 2024. (Saturday)

In my childhood, I often used to glance toward Hoor Ain's balcony as I came back from her house, but nobody was ever there. Today, instead of looking back, I headed straight to Mama's flat after finishing the work I had set out to do. Mama was telling me that he wanted me to teach Mami how to drive a car. I agreed, but I insisted that he come along too.

He said, "I have work to do; some guests are coming, and I need to meet them."

"Which guests?" I asked.

"They're coming to Zahra's house," he replied.

Who could these guests be, whom Mama deemed it necessary to meet? I started thinking. Maybe they're the same people Mama was talking to Huzaifa(Hoor Ain's brother) about regarding Hoor Ain's marriage proposal. Nobody told me anything, but I understood. Someone is coming for a marriage proposal to Hoor Ain, or we can call it my death proposal.

With each passing thought, my heartbeats are quickening, a strange sensation engulfing me. I can barely type, but I must maintain the facade of normalcy; I can't confide my restlessness to anyone, nor can I even think of doing so. And I'll try my best to appear normal; after all, this had to happen someday. It's been two hours since Mama went to Zahra aunt's house. Part of me wants to flee far away, but for now, I'll endure a little longer, and see what happens until Mama returns. So, I wait for Mama's return for two hours, pacing back and forth, waiting at the edge of my seat, sipping on tea and puffing one cigarette after another. I hope Mama will come back and reveal the outcome.

I'm anxiously waiting for Mama, but instead, he's summoned me to Zahra Aunt's house. I tried making excuses not to go, but none sufficed, and Mama insisted, "Come, have a cup of tea, and then you can leave; everyone is at Baji's house." When he called me so persistently, I had to go.

Upon arrival, the table was filled with snacks and cookies, perhaps all this food was prepared for the guests who had come to see Hoor Ain. Although there was plenty before me, I had no appetite. After much insistence, I picked up a date, but it was difficult to swallow it down.

Hoor Ain said, "Is the tea lacking of sugar?" I replied, "It's okay." She added more sugar and asked if it was better now.

No matter how much sugar she adds, this tea will always taste bitter to me, I whispered in my mind.

It's incredibly challenging to fake laughter, to behave normally when there's a raging fire inside, but I acted well, pretending to be normal. No one even suspected my forced laughter.

For one last time, I looked at her. Her fate is sealed now, and even if it isn't, it will be somewhere else, someday.

This was just their first meeting with those guests, and I wish it would be the last. no one mentioned anything in front of me, but everything was apparent. Hoor Ain was well dressed and their house was sharped clean which tells a complete story, and the most important thing was that she seemed happy, so let her be happy now. Whether it happens today or tomorrow, whether it's there or somewhere else, her alliance will be fixed, and then one day, there will be a wedding. I must strengthen myself from now on. I won't look back at her anymore; now, I must do what I have to do for myself and my parents. She never loved me, nor does she now, and perhaps she never will. All I know is that I just need to stay away from her now; I can't bear to see her with someone else right in front of my eyes.

I know it will be very difficult not to come in front of her, not to wander around her, and it will be very difficult to go far away from her. After all, the relationship is such that she is my Kala's daughter, and if I never go to their house, what will people think? But now, whoever needs to understand, let them understand; I won't put myself in trouble worrying about what people think or understand. I have to forget Hoor Ain. I was thinking that when I start earning 1 or 2 lakh rupees monthly, I could send a marriage proposal for Hoor Ain, but someone else came before that. And anyway, what guarantee do I have that I will ever earn that much money? So just forget about her. I know I can give Hoor Ain that love, that importance, that respect that no one else can give but I can't offer her big cars, big houses, bank balances, or a high status because I simply don't have all that; if I did, I would give it all to her. I want to see her happy but with me. If she's not with me, I don't want to see her at all. That's why I won't ever look at her now.

After every sorrow comes happiness, and after every difficulty comes relief. Everything doesn't come to a halt just because one person leaves. If it's destined by God, it will come to fruition.

I shouldn't cry over what I didn't get but rather be grateful for what I have.

27th February, 2024. (Tuesday)

It's been 3 days now, haven't spoken to her or seen her picture, but I couldn't free myself from her thoughts even for a moment. An invitation came yesterday to Zahra aunt's house; it's a gathering for everyone, including us. Now, one by one, all my Mother's sisters will invite Mama, and along with him, everyone, meaning all the relatives from my maternal side, will be invited. But I have to stay strong in my resolve. I'll make any excuse to delay or go somewhere else, but I won't go to her house. I will not go to the place where she would be present.

28th February, 2024. (Wednesday)

Everyone has already left for Abul Fazal, I said to my Mom I'll come later, but I'm still at home, and I don't even want to go there. It's already 6:45 PM, but I haven't received any calls yet. I hope Mom will call, and if she asks, I'll say, "I have a class today, so I won't be able to come."

Today, I'll manage to avoid going, but tomorrow, there will be a gathering at Mama's house, and I'll have to come up with a different excuse for that.

I enjoy it when there's a get-together, and everyone laughs and jokes together, but I know what will happen if I see her again. That's why it's better if I stay home alone.

The whole gathering is there, and I'm alone here. Only I know what I'm going through.

29th February, 2024. (Thursday)

As I mentioned, there's a gathering at Mama's house today at 6:30 in the evening. Everyone at home is getting ready to leave. I've also taken out my clothes and had them pressed by Mom. But when it's time to go, I'll make an excuse. Before that, no one should suspect my intentions.

I've told everyone to leave, saying I'll join after my class until 9 o'clock. Everyone has left, and my plan now is to go straight to Javed's flat from here. I'll tell Mom that a friend had an accident, so I had to go to him.

I don't like lying, but nowadays, I've started lying. I wish I could tell the truth, about why I can't go with you, but I don't want to cause trouble by mentioning Hoor Ain's name.

Has the time come when instead of finding reasons to meet her, I'm making excuses to stay away?

Mom called, asking why I hadn't arrived yet. I told her "I am going to Javed's flat; his health was very bad, and there was no one else with him." I've reached Javed's flat now. Javed is cooking biryani. Ibrar is exercising, and Sayyad has probably gone for a Rapido ride as a driver.

My upset face was telling a story, I shared everything with Javed and Ibrar about Hoor Ain's marriage proposal.

Javed says, "Don't worry, my brother. Surely, God must have written someone better for you."

Ibrar said "This is all about money, you used to say even with a salary of Rs.25,000 to Rs.30,000, one can live a peaceful life happily. Now, you see and tell me, Is it possible? it's all about money my friend"

I replied "You're right in your way, but in all this, it's not her fault. She never loved me, nor did she deceive me. But, Yes, I agree, everything would have been easier if I had money."

Tahzeeb Hafiz's lines came to mind when he said that.

Meri gurbat ne mujhse meri zindagi cheen li.....

Meri Amma to kahti thi Paisa kuch nahi hota...

In today's time, the importance of being in a girl's life is felt more when all our friends are busy on calls with their respective girlfriends, and we're left sitting alone like fools.

1st March, 2024. (Friday)

It's 11 AM, and I've returned home, but Mom and Dad, everyone is still at Abdul Fazal. Today, there's a lunch and dinner invitation at Aunt Samina's house. I've been called again, and now I have no other excuse not to go. This game of invitations has to stop now. I've already said I'll come after Friday prayers. First, I said I had a class, then I made an excuse about Javed's health. Now, I have no other excuse for not to go.

I don't understand what to do now. I'll have to go and face Hoor Ain. Why did Mom even need to arrange a dinner invitation there? If Mom had hosted it at our house, I wouldn't have to go there. If she had come to our house, I could have avoided going out, but now, how will I stay away from her there?

Finally, I had to go, but now I'll try not to look at her at all.

As soon as I arrived, everyone bombarded me with questions: "Have you come?" "Did you get time to come?" "Where were you yesterday?" and so on. And Aunt Zahra scolded me for not coming, but now, what does she know? She's scolding me for not coming on her invitation about the day before yesterday, now how can I say the reason.

When I went there, I didn't even look at Hoor Ain. I didn't even go to the room where she was present. When she came close, I lowered my gaze, but at the end, what I feared happened. I left home with Abdul Azeem my cousin, and when I returned, I saw everyone going to the park for an evening stroll at 7 PM. I refused to go, but Shiraz Mama caught hold of me and pulled me, and then even Hoor Ain held my hand. Mama and Hoor Ain both held my hand, pulling me to go with them.

How can someone be so innocent, or should I say foolish? I mean, she didn't understand that I wasn't looking at her, not talking to her, trying to avoid her, but she just came and held my hand as if nothing had happened. She doesn't even realize that for the past two days, I've been missing invitations because of her, just so I can stay away from her.

Or maybe I'm the fool who can't express his love or anger. Neither can I express that I want to stay away from her, nor can I express that I want to live with her.

All the determination I had built up over the past six days melted in six seconds when she held my hand. Now, I can't even stop myself from going with her. In the park, we all, Mom, Aunties, Mama, cousins, Hoor Ain, and I had a good time. We returned home by 9:00 PM, had dinner, and by midnight, everyone had returned to their homes.

Now, can someone tell me what to do in this situation? Earlier I did not want to go there, but later I did not want to come back home. I just don't want to get used to those joys that can never be mine.

I shouldn't forget that she was very happy the day those marriage proposals came for her. What happened to those proposals, whether they were accepted or not, I don't know. Hopefully, they must have been canceled by now, if God wills it. But I've returned to the same track I was trying to avoid.

2nd March, 2024. (Saturday)

The party, party, and more parties, they just don't seem to end. It's Razi's wedding now. Razi is my cousin from my paternal side. Today is the haldi ceremony, tomorrow is the wedding procession, and the day after tomorrow will be the reception. Maybe Hoor Ain won't come to the Haldi ceremony today.

Zahra aunt has arrived, but Hoor Ain is nowhere to be seen.

What a strange person I am.

My eyes search for her whom I don't want to see.

(Meri ankhe bhi wo chara dhundti hen jise me dekhna nahi chata)

She didn't come, and I feel no interest in this gathering.

4th March, 2024. (Monday)

Today is the reception, but before that, there's a lunch invitation at Shahzad Mama's house. They live in Jaitpur near my house the same nani's hourse, and the wedding reception is also in Jaitpur. It was around 3:30 in the afternoon when I arrived at Mama's house, and Hoor Ain was already there. We had lunch together.

After lunch, when everyone was seated (all the aunts, mama, cousins, and Hoor Ain), the topic of my marriage came up. Every time the topic of my marriage arises, all the relatives only see one girl for me, and that's "Kinza". I've refused many times, but they still keep asking me for the reasons for my refusal and questioning me about it. Again they started the questions.

"What is lacking in that girl?" Aunt asked.

"What is the reason for your refusal?" Someone asked.

"The girl is also good, and you'll also get 50 lakh rupees as a dowry, so why don't you agree?" Mama asked jokingly with a real fact.

"If you like some other girl, then tell us?" One more question from the audience.

While everyone else's questions were on one side, I was most troubled by Hoor Ain's questions when she too was asking the same questions as everyone else. I wanted Hoor Ain to be jealous, but she was enjoying herself thoroughly. If the topic of Hoor Ain's marriage came up in front of me, I would feel burning inside

In the end, I said this much, "If I were to say that I like someone else, then you all would leave me alone, right?"

To this, Hoor Ain responded, "No! Then you'll have to tell us her name whom you like."

I started thinking to myself, "She's asking for a name, that she owns, Yes it's you. If I were to speak her name, it would stir up a storm here, and everyone would get their answer all at once."

Everyone was asking questions, but I remained silent, with no response to anyone's words.

Perhaps I should have spoken up, I love a girl that I do not deserve, I love a girl who does not love me, and I love a girl whose name is Hoor Ain. Now will you guys still worry about my happiness? Now will you guys still help me? And now you don't have the answers to my questions.

I didn't say anything to anyone; I switched the topic.

By 9:00 PM, we all arrived at the reception.

I brought Hoor Ain and her Mom, in the car. As soon as I stopped the car in front of the banquet hall, I opened the car door for Hoor Ain, just like a hero, these small things have made me happy since childhood.

After parking the car, I headed to the banquet hall. Around 11:00 PM, With an excuse of finding my mother, I went to the ladies department to see Hoor Ain, it had been quite a while since I had seen her. I saw her from a distance; she was talking and smiling in a group. Her smiling face serves as therapy for me. Her smiling face was right in front of me, and suddenly I remembered the day when people came for her proposal. A strange restlessness, an odd fear, an unusual feeling gripped me. I fear what will happen if she isn't mine, what will become of me if she belongs to someone else. I am terrified at the thought that one day she will marry someone else. My anxiety grew, I couldn't approach her, nor could I speak to her, and now she has gone home, while I returned to mine. But I still feel that same restlessness. Anyway, I shouldn't think too much; it's late at night, so I should sleep now. Good night.

Chapter - 5

Open Mike Performance

6th March, 2024. (Wednesday)

Today, at around 2:00 PM, I took my bike from home for my first Rapido ride to earn some money since I am financially challenged these days. I returned home around 6:00 PM, and today's total earnings were Rs 95, but the petrol cost me Rs 100, so the entire time was wasted and a heavy loss of Rs 5. Now, I'll probably go to another location tomorrow, maybe I'll earn something there. The first day as a Rapido driver was a waste; let's see what happens tomorrow.

10th March, 2024. (Saturday)

I have Hoor Ain's WhatsApp number, and I also have her Instagram ID, my heart also wants me to talk to her, but I don't have any reason or excuse to talk. The day before yesterday, I went to Abul Fazal, and I had a little chat with Hoor Ain. I told her that these days I was driving a Rapido bike, at first, she was shocked to hear that, but then I shared my entire Rapido experience with her, just two days' worth. After a while, she asked me which classes I was taking these days. I proudly told her, "Data Scientist".

I always worry that if I don't become successful soon, Hoor Ain will get married somewhere else. I can't ask for time from anyone. I'm disturbed by this thought these days. I think if I can't do something now, I won't be able to do anything later. No one but God can make my difficulties easier. But the best thing is that Ramadan is coming. The day after tomorrow will be the first fast.

Let me share an experience with you today. About 4 years ago, I wrote poetry for someone, obviously for Hoor Ain. But I couldn't say it in front of her, but I dared to say it in front of the whole world. So, I went to a studio, an open mic studio called "Poem and Kahaniyan". When I arrived there, I saw a hall with about 30 people sitting on the carpet, all facing toward the stage and waiting for a poet to come. On the stage, there was a mic and a chair with a black background curtain.

There was a cameraman in front, ready to record everything. Most of the audience had a piece of paper in their hands, on which their sorrow was written, and these people called their sorrow "poetry". Whenever someone's name was called, they would come up on stage with their paper and recite their poetry. People would applaud to appreciate them, but I was only clapping so that they would clap for me too. These people were poets, but the only difference between them and real poets was that real poets charge money for reciting poetry, but these people had come to recite poetry by paying money. After all, I had also paid Rs. 500 to record my poetry.

When my name was announced, I also took my paper and went up on stage. Nervously, I opened my paper and began to recite the poetry I had written.

"Meri khuwahish"
Is saste se kagaz per badi mahangi
shayari likhkar laya hun.....
Apko pasand Ho ya Na Ho lekin
sacchi likh kar aaya hun...
Arz kya hai gor farmaen.
Kab tu duaon mein mangi mujhe
Jaise main mangta hun....
kab tu raaton Ko jagegi meri yad
mein jaise me jagta hun.....
Kab mere aansu girne se pahle tere nain bheeg jaenge...
kab mere muskurane se hi tere ashq sukh jaenge....
Kab aayegi wo subah jab aankh
khulate hi Tera chehra samne paunga.....
kab beetegi wo raat jab tujhe dekhta dekhta hi so jaunga....
Kab tujhe mohobbat hogi mujhse jese me karta hun....
Kab tu samjhegi me tujhpe kitna martaa hun....

Kab hakeekat karegi tu un khwabo ko Jo Mai apni ankho me sajata hun ...
Kab tasalli degi is dil ko jise me Roz bahkata hun....
Kab meri khwahish ko tu karegi pura...
Ya mera pyar rah jayga Umar bhar adhura....
Kab mere andhere khwabo me tu karegi ujala.....
Kab tere Bhai ko tu banaygi mera sala....
Ya tutenge sare khwab or rah jayga andera..
Or le jayga koi or use jo pyar hai sirf mera...
Bohot Darr lagta hai us din se jo ek din samne aayga...
Mai bachpan se chahta hu jise use koi or le jayga...
Or akhri Shairy kah kar khatam karna chahunga....
Ek ek aansu ko apni aankho mei kaid karke rakha hai mene inki rihai ke faisle Teri bidai Wale din kar dunga....
Thank you.

People applauded, and the performance ended, but now the real game would begin when Hoor Ain watched this video. I didn't mention her name, but she will probably understand, and after watching the video, she'll come running to me and hug me, saying, "I am sorry Faizan, I realized it too late, but now I am all yours, will you marry me?" When she says it with so much love, I will also angrily wipe away my tears.

I uploaded the video on my YouTube channel but didn't personally share it. Then someone shared the link of that video in a WhatsApp group where I and Hoor Ain were also members. Everyone praised the video, but there was no response from Hoor Ain. I don't know if she even watched the video or not. Perhaps she never watched it, and even if she did, it wouldn't have mattered to her. Maybe I was just over-excited for no reason.

After some time, I once again went to the same platform and shared poetry summarizing my love story. But perhaps she didn't watch that second video either, nor did she ever talk about it. However, other relatives kept asking who the girl was for whom I was writing poetry. Well, it's been four years now, and everyone seems to have forgotten about these things, but I can never forget that person who never remembers me.

Anyway, let's meet after Eid. I'll stop writing in this diary for now and start again after Eid.

Wait for the part - 2

www.ingramcontent.com/pod-product-compliance
Lightning Source LLC
LaVergne TN
LVHW041636070526
838199LV00052B/3385